D0118785

This Special Edition of *The Yanov Torah*
has been printed to honor the celebration of
Jaden Amanda Yonover
as a Bat Mitzvah.

April 26, 2014

The Yonover Family would like to thank
Mrs. Agnes Herman for granting permission to
reprint this important work, which she authored
with her late husband, Rabbi Erwin Herman.
We would also like to thank Rabbi Richard Levy
and the Hebrew Union College, who so
generously allowed Jaden to read from
The Yanov Torah on this very special day.

We would also like to honor the memory of those
who so bravely insured the existence of
The Yanov Torah and Judaism – and
who understood that defiance and victory
can take many forms.

Never Forget.

THE YANOV TORAH

By Erwin and Agnes Herman
Illustrated by Katherine Janus Kahn

KAR-BEN COPIES, INC.   ROCKVILLE, MD

Portions of The Yanov Torah *first appeared in* Moment *magazine.*

Library of Congress Cataloging in Publication Data

Herman, Erwin.
    The Yanov Torah.

    Summary: Jews in a work camp in Yanov during the Nazi occupation of L'vov,
Poland, smuggle in a Torah, piece by piece, despite enormous personal danger.
    1. Children's stories, American. [1. Torah scrolls—Fiction. 2. Poland—History—
Occupation, 1939-1945—Fiction. 3. World War, 1939-1945—Jews—Fiction. 4. Jews—
Poland—Fiction] I. Herman, Agnes. II. Kahn, Katherine, ill. III. Title.
PZ7.H43138Yan   1985   [Fic]   85-5269
ISBN 0-930494-45-8
ISBN 0-930494-46-6 (pbk.)

Published by KAR-BEN COPIES, INC., Rockville, MD
Printed in the United States of America

To Joyce and Lee Goldin,
for providing new life to the Yanov Torah

L'VOV 1978

This story does not begin with "once upon a time." I know exactly when it began—at 2:30 p.m., the afternoon of October 28, 1978. How can I be so certain? Because this is MY story.

Emanuel Orlove is my name. I am a 31-year-old doctor. I live in Los Angeles, my newly-adopted city, with my wife Esther, and our two children, Alexander, aged 8, and Maia, who is only 3.

Until three months ago, we were residents of L'vov, a large city in Eastern Europe. If you ask, "In what country is L'vov?", expect a variety of answers. My hometown has had more owners than a used car! Before World War II, it was part of Poland. Then the Nazis took it over, and in 1944, Russia captured the area from the Nazis. So, from the time I was born, the USSR had been my home. And it was that home I planned to leave when, on October 28, 1978, at 2:30 p.m., my wife and I began our walk to "OVIR," the Soviet Government Office, to apply for emigration.

In the breast pocket of my jacket was a letter from my sister Elana, inviting us to join her in Los Angeles. Without that letter we could just as well have stayed home. The Soviet government is not eager to allow anyone to leave the country, so it has a strict set of rules. A letter of invitation from a close family member in America or Israel is the first step for a Jew wanting to leave.

Even with the letter, I was not confident. The Russians do not make it easy to leave. If you get past all the obstacles they create, the Soviets may simply say, "Nyet!" And that is that.

Inside the office door, Esther and I took our places at the end of a long line of restless men and women. We were gripped by fears and doubts. We were natives of L'vov; Russia was the only homeland we had known. We had been educated in the city's schools, housed in its apartments, cared for by its medical program. Esther had been trained as a civil engineer in the local university; I had received my medical degree there. We were employed by the government, highly respected in our jobs, and proud of our accomplishments.

Leaving raised a host of concerns. As Jews, we were no longer comfortable in our homeland. We feared that

our decision would insult the government and offend our friends and neighbors. For many days, these questions lay unanswered alongside our emigration papers. Finally, we took courage and submitted the forms. A week later, I was fired from my position at the hospital.

===

GRANDPA

Permission to leave was slow in coming. When the exit papers arrived 16 months later, our excitement was hard to contain. The instructions were precise. We were to leave the country in two weeks, exactly. There was so much to do.

First, Grandpa had to be called. Grandpa Orlove was very special to all of us. He had lived in Moscow all his life, and nothing we could do or say would persuade him to move to L'vov. Though he was 80 years old, Grandpa visited us twice each year; we went to Moscow twice, in return. Grandpa supported our desire to leave, but we knew he would not be coming with us.

He was waiting for our call. I explained the details of our departure. We had only two weeks, and we wanted Grandpa to spend them with us.

He required no convincing. "The train schedule has been posted on the refrigerator for months," he said. "I will arrive tomorrow afternoon at 3:43. Don't be late!" The phone clicked off. For Grandpa Orlove, further conversation was unnecessary.

During breakfast, on the second day of his visit, Grandpa asked me to take him to see an old friend who lived on the other side of the city. I was pleased to go with him; it gave us a few extra hours together.

THE TAXI took us to a decayed and crumbling section of L'vov. We located the apartment house and, slowly, climbed three flights of rotting, wooden stairs. Grandpa knocked persistently on the door of Apartment 320 until finally a feeble voice invited us in.

Bright sunshine greeted us, illuminating both an almost barren room and a gaunt, old man. He lay in an ancient, cast iron bed and did not stir as we entered the room. Grandpa Orlove walked around the bed and bent over his friend. "It's Orlove, Sasha Orlove; I've come from Moscow to see you, dear friend!" The old man managed a weak smile. He reached out to Grandpa, and the two men embraced.

The lump in my throat left me speechless. When Grandpa finally remembered to introduce me, I could only nod and smile. They did not notice; old friends have much to say to one another.

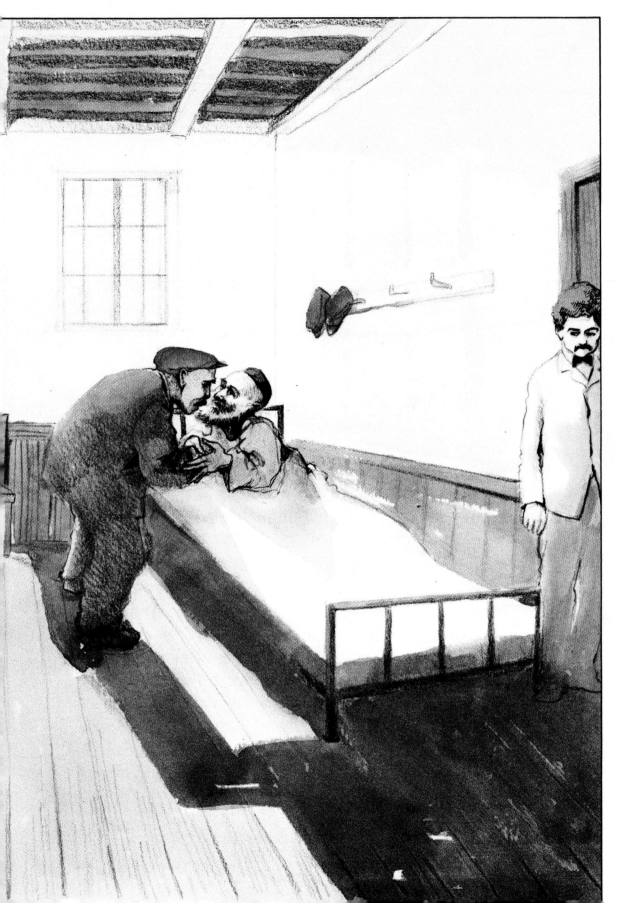

Actually, Grandpa did most of the talking. He regaled his friend with recollections of experiences they had shared many years before. At times, his friend bobbed his head in agreement; at times, he hugged his thin body, shaking with uncontrollable laughter. Suddenly, there was silence. The old man, exhausted from remembering and laughing, lay back against his pillow. Grandpa lifted himself unsteadily from his kneeling position, groaned a little as he flexed his arthritic knees, and sat gratefully on the chair I had moved into place.

THE MOMENT had come to reveal the real reason for our visit. "My children are going away," Grandpa began, and with funereal cadence, recited the plans we had made to leave L'vov. "In less than ten days I shall say goodbye to Emanuel here—to all of them—for the last time, you can be sure." Grandpa was melancholy. The old man on the bed lifted his head unsteadily and nodded. He had compassion for his sorrowing friend.

Grandpa continued, "You are a good person, my friend, a fine Jew. A *mensch*. Emanuel needs your blessing. For my sake, will you bless him?"

I opened my mouth to protest. A blessing was not what I needed; I needed luck! But I could not deny Grandpa. It was difficult for him to watch us go; perhaps it would help to send us off with special blessings.

The old man was silent as he dragged his body into a sitting position. He refused my offer of help. In obvious pain, he moved his legs around to the side of the bed and slowly lowered them to the floor. With one hand gripping Grandpa's shoulder and the other pressed against the wall, he pushed and pulled himself upright. He disengaged himself and, without a word, limped out of the room.

FOR LONG MINUTES, Grandpa and I stared at the door. When the old man reappeared, he was clutching a Torah, hugged to his chest. I rushed to help. He shrugged me aside and moved toward the bed, where he gently deposited the scroll. He bent over it, stroked it lovingly, seeming to forget we were there. Then he untied its binding and spread apart the wooden staves, revealing the faded, brown script. Pointing a bony index finger at the parchment, he began a sing-song chant. *"B'rayshees bara..."* I did not understand. Grandpa whispered to me, "...the first words of the Holy Scriptures." The thin voice continued reverently. Then it stopped. The old man sank heavily to the bed, alongside the Torah.

Minutes passed. Color returned to his cheeks. He crooked his right forefinger to beckon us close. "This...is the...Yanov Torah!" He spoke slowly, savoring each word. "There is no other Torah like this in all the world. It is proof of *t'chiyas hamayseem*, of God's ability to bring the dead back to life!" I listened, without understanding.

The old man rose once more, strength miraculously renewed. Inviting Grandpa to hold fast to one wooden

stave while he rolled the parchment onto the other, he urged me to come closer. Once more he pointed to the script. "See...how different the writing is...look here...look there...one *amud*, one column only; that is not the proper way for a Torah. There should be at least four columns to a *klaf*, a section of parchment. And a Torah must be clean and nice. Not like our Yanov Torah." His words were without criticism. He seemed proud that this Torah was flawed, even pleased with its unattractiveness.

I was impatient for details, but once again Grandpa's old friend sat down to catch his breath. He was marshalling his strength to tell us a long and important story.

YANOV 1941

Rested, the old man began the story of the Yanov Torah.

When Hitler—may his name be erased—wanted to kill us, he sent soldiers to our beautiful city of L'vov. They looked over our fine young people and decided that they were strong enough to work for the Nazi's Third Reich." The last words were bitter on his tongue.

"So they built a camp in nearby Yanov—a 'work camp' they called it. They drove into it every Jew from this part of the country who could wield an axe or a shovel. The rest—the very old and the sick and the handicapped—were allowed to stay home, without jobs, without their families, without medical help. It was a horror, a terror.

"The Jews who remained in L'vov did not openly complain. They knew that their limited freedom was a thousand times better than the slavery of the camp. Once a week, they traveled to Yanov to share with the imprisoned members of their families the little they still possessed. The guards encouraged them. The sacks of food, clothing, books, and toilet articles provided booty and bounty to be confiscated for their own enjoyment. And who dared argue? When the guards had taken their fill, what little remained sometimes got to the prisoners. In Yanov, a little was a lot, so the gifts and packages continued.

"ONE DAY, six of our men were informed that, because of good behavior, they could return home for 24 hours. Can you imagine the excitement! They couldn't believe it! Of course, each had a brother, sister, child, or parent remaining in the camp: insurance that the men would return. The guards knew that no one would risk the fate of a loved one; the six men knew that the guards would not hesitate to punish their family members.

"We later learned that this brief freedom was an act unheard of in camps elsewhere. God only knows why we were so lucky. Spirits in Yanov soared. In L'vov, behind drawn shades, six reunited families were delirious with joy.

"Before the end of the 24 hours, the six freed Jews had returned to camp, hopeful that their good behavior would encourage the authorities to continue the visits home. To help convince them further, the inmates brought back sweets and gifts which, of course, were confiscated by the greedy guards.

"Six weeks later, excitement returned to the prison community. The procedure was to be repeated. This time, 24 men were allowed to return to their families.

"IT WAS DURING this second visit that two of the men revealed a remarkable story: every day, in the darkness of the barracks, religious services were being conducted in secret. Jews who knew the prayers by heart taught them to those who didn't. Starved by their captors, fatigued by labor, they still found the strength to *daven* together daily. Now, they wanted a Torah!

"'Impossible!' everyone agreed. The Nazis had plundered the synagogues for religious articles. They would never allow such a thing! The whole idea was too dangerous.

"Several of our leaders, determined to be helpful, met with the rabbis. They debated the request for a long,

long time. Finally, a decision was reached. Word of it was whispered from house to house. The sacred Torahs, which had been buried in the Jewish cemetery when trouble was imminent, would be dug up; their parchments would be separated, and piece by piece, they would be smuggled into Yanov.

"For some of our people, the news was exhilarating. For others, devastating! The debate raged: Why take such a risk? The whole visitation program could be destroyed. Our sons and brothers could be executed! It was dangerous...daring...magnificent!

"The rabbis made the decision: each man, home on a pass, would be given the opportunity to volunteer as a carrier, or to refuse. There would be no recriminations.

"The plan was struck! It was time to begin! The first man to volunteer stepped forward."

YANOV 1942

Once more, Grandpa's friend paused for breath. This time, he shut his eyes and dropped his chin on his chest. I wondered if he would be able to continue. Moments passed, and again he picked up the thread of his astonishing story.

Moshe was his name; Moshe, the tailor, was the first to volunteer. He was a quiet man, who spoke with a stammer, so he did not often have a lot to say. Moshe was deeply religious and very clever. No one was surprised when he leaped forward, and no one was surprised that he already had devised a way to smuggle in the Torah.

"Moshe would not share the details. He asked only to be left alone with the stacks of separated parchments. Obediently, the rabbis and elders filed out of the room. In a few moments, Moshe called them back.

"NOTHING APPEARED CHANGED. The stacks of parchments did not seem smaller; Moshe was the same, except that he had about him an almost mischievous look. Moshe began to unbutton his shirt, slowly, deliberately, and a creamy white parchment appeared. He had bound it skillfully around his body, the sacred words pressed to his flesh. When he rebuttoned his shirt, it disappeared. The men walked around him, beside him, before him, and behind him. They saw only shirt. They made him walk, sit, stand, turn, as they checked him thoroughly with piercing eyes. Convinced that no one would ever suspect him of being wrapped in the precious parchment, they broke into applause. Moshe had found a way. Of course, everyone understood that the big test would come at the Yanov gate: could Moshe fool the guards as he had fooled them? In less than 24 hours they would know.

"The rabbis showered him with blessings, the elders with words of encouragement. They knew that they had to build Moshe's confidence along with their own. They paced and worried. Some renewed their early arguments

against the idea; second thoughts crowded in. They could all be punished for one misstep. But Moshe was glowing with excitement. He seemed to be preparing himself for a kind of contest. Suddenly, everyone understood: Moshe was going to war; the tailor was taking on the Nazis! David would battle Goliath!

"The elders prepared three packages: cakes and sweets, a new pair of shoes that came from who-knows-where, and as always, a few books. If the greedy guards were kept busy, they might not notice Moshe's awkward posture.

"WHEN MOSHE APPROACHED Yanov and saw the sign over the main gate, he laughed to himself. 'Work Creates Freedom.' What a desecration of the word freedom! But he quickly turned his attention to the two guards at the gate. They were heavily armed. Their rifle barrels glistened in the sunshine. They looked ugly, angry.

"Shifting his packages to ease the tension in his shoulders, Moshe presented his identification papers. The shorter guard snatched them out of his hand, then grunted to his colleague who swung open the heavy, iron gate. Moshe was ordered to move on. He had reached the crucial moment. One false move and they would search him. His heart pounded against the parchment.

"THE THREE GUARDS seated at the table never lifted their eyes. 'Packages on the table, Jew!' The words were fired at Moshe like so many sharp darts. Stiff with strain and sick with fear, he dropped his packages on the long, wooden table. One of the paper sacks split, spilling its contents onto the table and ground. The thieving guards reached down and grabbed for their loot, then appraised it. Moshe shifted his weight from one foot to the other. He coughed nervously.

"One of the soldiers picked up a new shoe that had fallen from the sack, turned it round and round in his hand, eyed it suspiciously, then rose slowly from his chair. With his eyes fixed on the tailor, he moved with catlike grace around the table. Moshe began to panic. His mind commanded him to run; his legs would not move.

"The soldier stood before him, menacingly. He lifted his arms slowly, and with a quick downward movement, gripped Moshe's shoulders, pressuring them with iron-strong fingers until the tailor's knees buckled and he slumped to the ground.

"MOSHE SAW the hobnail boot as it began its arc. Later, he would recall with slow-motion accuracy the polished toe that reflected sunlight at the moment it struck his chest. He tumbled backwards until his head crashed into the table. Like a discarded rag doll, he slumped to the ground, his arms and legs twisted gro-

tesquely. There was no pain now, only darkness—deep, cavernous darkness.

"MOSHE AWAKENED in his own bunk in the barracks. He tried to breathe deeply, but gasped in pain from the impact of the boot. The faces of his friends came into focus and comforted him. Suddenly, he remembered his mission and with frantic fingers tore at the buttons of his shirt. The sacred parchment appeared, wrapped about his body. Moshe grinned through his tears. The Torah had entered Yanov!

"When the guards heard the cheer from the tailor's barracks, they were too busy with their bounty to investigate. 'Crazy Jews,' one said, and the rest laughed in agreement."

FREEDOM

I was so absorbed by the story of courage and faith that I jumped when Grandpa poked me to get my attention. His friend was coughing uncontrollably and needed a drink of water. As I held the glass to his lips, I begged the old man to rest. We would wait; he could finish the story later. He protested and motioned me to sit down again. The coughing subsided, and he continued.

At Yanov we worked hard, very hard. We were the slaves of an insane master. Many died—oh, so many died. There were times when we thought they were the lucky ones. We were starved, beaten, cursed. Always we were expected to work. There was no place in Yanov for those who were too weak or sick to work any longer. Each week, they were lined up and herded

31

into trucks. The camp orchestra, our own families and friends, had to play German songs while these trucks took our people away. The guards assured us that the sick were going to a special hospital for care, but we knew better. We had no proof then, but we knew better.

"ONE JUNE MORNING in 1945, we awakened to a strange silence. The wake-up siren had not sounded. No guards cursed or shouted or laughed. No one banged on our doors. It was a frightening silence. We spoke quietly in the barracks and agreed to open the door just a crack. The courtyard was empty, deserted. I volunteered to walk outside. I tested each step as if I were in a mine field. All of a sudden, I heard a terrible noise. I raced back into the room. 'Did you hear it? A thousand motors! They're coming to take all of us!'

"With a crash, our barracks door burst open. Russian soldiers entered, their rifles pointed. One of our group cried out, 'Don't kill us; we're slaves, Nazi prisoners.' He paused, and then in a calmer, dignified voice added, 'We are Jews.' The Russian Commander, looking around with disbelief at the hundreds of pale, skinny, trapped men, said simply, 'And you are free.'

"At that exquisite moment of liberation, I did not think about the Torah. Even weeks later, when we were allowed to return to camp to claim our few belongings, I did not think of it. I had only one thought: I was alive!

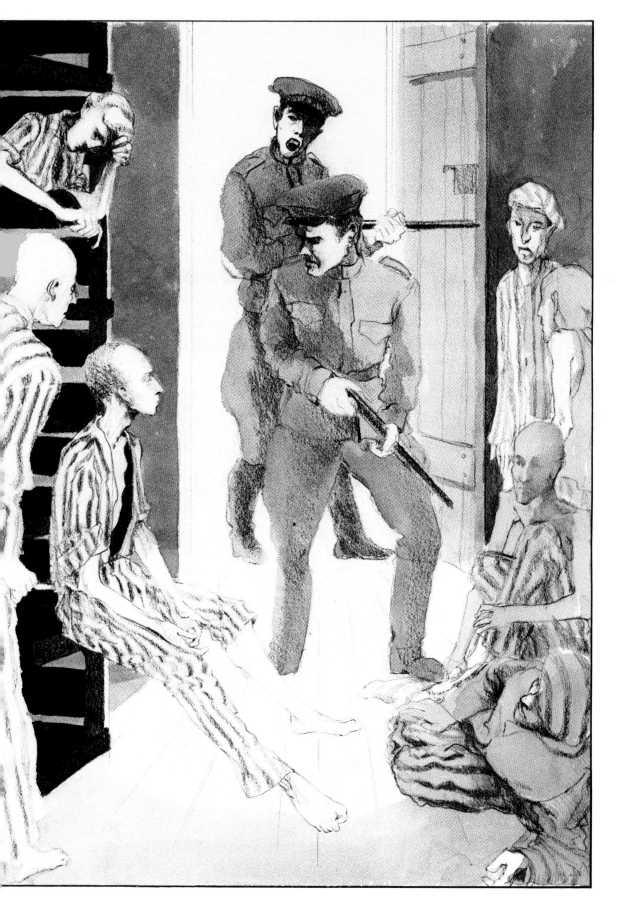

"ONE DAY I learned that Moshe had been travelling through L'vov, speaking with inmates from as many of the barracks as he could find, asking all of them the same question: 'Where are your parchments hidden?' The ingenuity with which the prisoners had hidden the parchments was unbelievable. Moshe told me about the hollow rails of the bedposts; the loose brick behind our sink; the holes in the floor, lined with old shirts and covered with dirt. He had uncovered and collected dozens of Torah pieces from their hiding places.

"MONTHS LATER, I attended a very special community meeting. The handful of us who had not fled L'vov after liberation met to discuss our future. We had agreed that we would not spend any time dwelling on the horrors of the past. Each of us was in mourning. As survivors, we had a great need to move ahead with our lives. We were a small, pitiful number. So many wonderful friends were gone, murdered."

Grandpa's friend paused again, tears streaming down his face. Grandpa reached over and patted his hand, in compassion and understanding.

"Sasha," the old man used Grandpa's name for the first time, "I come now to the most important part of my story! You must be patient a little while longer, and I will finish."

THE TORAH

Regaining his composure, the old man continued.

Just before the end of our meeting, our chairman announced, 'We are not Yanov's only survivors!' We looked at each other, then around the room, searching for late arrivals. There were none.

"Taking a bulky package from behind the rostrum, the chairman smiled for the first time and began unwrapping the bundle. 'My friends,' he said, and his voice broke, '...my dear friends, this precious survivor was created from remnants of the past, our past!' He lifted a Torah high above the table, then settled it lovingly in the crook of his arm.

35

"'THIS IS OUR Yanov Torah, pieced together by our brave friend Moshe. It is a sign and a memorial. Though so many of our friends were murdered by Hitler and his gang of hoodlums, our Torah lives. Now we, too, must piece together our lives—and live!'

"He lifted the Torah high above his head and shouted, *'Am Yisrael Chai!*—The people of Israel lives!' We sang and we cried and we hugged one another. Then, forming a circle around the Torah, we danced ecstatically. Once again, the Yanov Torah had given us hope!

"WHEN THE CHAIRMAN finally restored order, he asked how many of us planned to remain in L'vov. I raised my hand. Few others did. Most wanted to wipe out the past, to rebuild their lives elsewhere. Others were leaving in search of loved ones who might have survived.

"The chairman looked carefully at the few raised hands and called Isaac Levi forward. Before the Nazis came, Levi had owned the finest jewelry store in L'vov. In his youth he had been an athlete. The Nazis took advantage of his strength and worked him like an animal. That night at the meeting he limped forward, emaciated and pale. None of his former grace and athletic build was evident; at 60 he was, physically, a broken man.

"'You, Isaac Levi, are the oldest Jewish survivor remaining in L'vov,' the chairman said. 'So we are entrusting the Torah to your care.' Our chairman placed it in his arms.

"The jeweler was deeply moved. He embraced the Torah, then kissed it. 'I cherish this honor.' His voice, like his hands, trembled. 'I will protect our Torah with my life, and when I die, it shall be entrusted to the remaining oldest survivor of Yanov Camp. May we all live to be one hundred and twenty!'

"'*Bis ein hundert und tsvantsig,*' we shouted in reply. And we wept."

THE OLD MAN had finished his story. He rose from the bed once more, his spindly legs offering him little support. He lifted the Torah from the bed and asked me to stand.

"I am the last survivor of Yanov still living in L'vov, and this Torah has been in my care for the past 18 years. Take it, my son. Yes, take it with you to America. In America it will live!"

I felt a sense of awe as he placed the Yanov Torah in my arms. The Hebrew letters crudely embroidered on the bright blue cloth were meaningless to me, yet I felt their power. This Torah, which had survived so much, was now in my trust. Together, we would begin again in America.

But before America, the Torah would once again have to pass the guards, this time at the border gate!

DEPARTURE 1980

The day of departure arrived. There was so much to do and so many last minute goodbyes to be spoken. Everyone dressed warmly, for it was the end of February. We put extra sweaters, socks, and gloves on the children, and bundled ourselves in double layers of coats and pants. Each adult was permitted to carry one suitcase, but children were not allowed any luggage, except for one small toy. We knew we would have to leave most of our belongings behind, but the two-suitcase limit posed a very serious problem: what about the Torah? I would have to carry it separately. I worried that the Russians might decide it was an extra piece of luggage or that they might confiscate it. My heart raced at the thought of the confrontation at the border. As we got ready to leave, I lifted the Torah, testing its weight on my arm.

"Perhaps we should not take it," Esther hesitated. "It could get us into trouble. You know how mean the guards can be! Leave it, Emanuel. Please! Grandpa would understand."

40

Her fears echoed my own. But somehow I knew that if I protected the Torah, it would protect us. I answered Esther honestly. "I promised Grandpa and his friend; it is a trust. I shall bring the Torah to America." She said no more.

And so, turning our backs on our home forever, we boarded the bus for the first step of our journey. It was a long ride. I looked out at the streets of L'vov for the last time: the University, the hospital, the children's school, our shops and markets. I was both sad and hopeful.

WHEN WE CAME to the Czech border, the bus stopped and we were ordered out. Our papers would be examined before we could take yet another bus through Czechoslovakia on the way to Vienna and freedom.

Half a dozen huge, frowning men in Army uniforms stood, hands on hips, looking us up and down. I was tense and impatient.

The soldier standing nearest me grabbed the papers that I offered, then took his time reading them through. With my papers in hand, he disappeared into the little wooden shack that was his office. My heart stopped; I could not see what he was doing, but my imagination supplied frightening answers. After five long minutes he emerged, flicked a cigarette onto the ground, and handed back my papers. Sensing our fear, the guard had gone inside for a smoke. I hoped silently that this might be the only harassment.

Another officer motioned us to move on, then spied the blue-checkered bundle resting on our luggage. Esther had slipped the Torah into a pillowcase as we left the house.

"What's that? Open it! What are you trying to smuggle out of here?" I froze with fear. "Open it, or I will cut it open."

Quickly, I lifted the pillowcase while trying to explain its contents. I mumbled something about a family heirloom, a relic from the old days, valuable only to the family. I was not very coherent.

The guard grabbed the pillowcase like a sack of potatoes and carried the Torah into the shack. He made a phone call. Twenty minutes later, a dusty old auto pulled up alongside the shack. A serious looking man in a business suit got out and went inside. Through the window, we watched him examine the Torah. We shivered with fear and cold, and we waited. Would they take the Torah from us? Would they arrest us? Would they send us back? Esther never looked at me. We did not speak. Each of us held a child close, trying to be comforting and reassuring.

WHEN THE OFFICER and the stranger emerged, they were not smiling.

"Two hundred rubles," the officer announced. "It is worthless to us, just as you are. But it is extra luggage. You must pay."

Two hundred rubles was all the money the Russian authorities had permitted us to take out of the country to start our new lives in America. Now they were demanding even that—the final humiliation. I paid.

Exhausted, we climbed aboard the waiting bus. We were penniless, but we were free.

I had begun to fulfill my trust. The Yanov Torah was on its way to America. In America it would live.

EPILOGUE by Rabbi Erwin Herman

The Yanov Torah is now in my possession.

This happened as a result of the remarkable story you have just read. Several years ago, Dr. Emanuel Orlove (not his real name) walked into my office, with a bulky bundle under his arm. In broken English, he repeated a half request, half command: "You buy my Torah."

Orlove needed money desperately. He was not allowed to practice medicine until he passed his state licensing exam. He was working part-time as a hospital orderly, so he could learn English and study for the exam. The Torah was the only thing of value he possessed. Over the course of the next two hours, he told me the story of the Yanov Torah. I pleaded with Orlove to keep the Torah, and offered him financial help. He would not accept charity.

"I doctor!" he stated proudly.

The following day, I invited two friends, leaders in the Jewish community, to my office. I told them the story.

They offered to purchase the Torah for a generous sum. Dr. Orlove would be able to feed his family while he studied for his medical license.

And what of the Yanov Torah?

The benefactors' check for Dr. Orlove arrived with a letter. This is what it said:

Dear Rabbi,

We have purchased this Torah for you. It must not be given to a museum, for that would limit its purpose. We ask you to carry it from temple to temple, from place to place, wherever you travel in this world. Tell its story to Jews and non-Jews alike. Let it be understood by all, that although millions of Jews have been murdered, our Torah will live forever. The Yanov Torah testifies to that truth!

ABOUT THE AUTHORS

ERWIN HERMAN received his rabbinical ordination at the Hebrew Union College in Cincinnati, where he earned a Doctor of Divinity degree. After serving congregations in North Carolina and Pennsylvania, he joined the national staff of the Union of American Hebrew Congregations. During his 25-year tenure, he occupied a variety of national staff positions, most recently as Director of the Pacific Southwest Council. His stories and articles have been published in several Jewish magazines and history and sociology texts.

AGNES HERMAN earned a Masters' Degree in Social Work from Columbia University and worked as a caseworker, supervisor, and Director of Volunteers for family service agencies in Ohio, New York, and California. She edited a newsletter for the Los Angeles Family Service Center and writes a column on Judaism for the *San Marcos Courier*.

The publication of THE YANOV TORAH, the Hermans' first collaborative literary effort, coincides with the celebration of their 40th wedding anniversary. The couple has two children.

ABOUT THE ILLUSTRATOR

KATHERINE JANUS KAHN received her undergraduate degree in Humanities from the University of Chicago and studied Fine Arts at the Bezalel School in Jerusalem and the University of Iowa. In Jerusalem she rediscovered her Jewish heritage, and has devoted herself to illustrating an impressive list of Jewish books for children, including history and holiday books and, most recently, a set of board books for toddlers. Her drawings for *The Passover Parrot* and *The Odd Potato* (Kar-Ben) have been widely acclaimed. She lives in Wheaton, MD, with her husband David and son Bert.